INGER KIER

MATCH made in HEAVEN

Dedication to my deceased husband Lyle Kier

© 2016 Inger Kier
Publishing and printing: BoD
ISBN: 978-91-7699-012-4

I sit in the kitchen and looking at the beautiful sky with orange clouds and among these, I see airplanes as a string of pearls fly against the airport.

I wonder, if my beloved husband is among all these orange clouds.

Memories come to me of a beautiful, caring, supportive husband, who thinks of others before himself. He is always a courteous gentleman, pleasant against other people. He loved me so much. I was his "Precious Angel," his "Sweetheart", his "Honey". I will never hear these beautiful words anymore.

My beloved husband Dean died 06:15 am, on a cold February morning. His heart stopped three times.

2 days before I received a call from the hospital, that Dean's heart stopped, but they started it with CPR.

When I arrived the next morning at the hospital, I heard him say to me:

"Hey, I thought, you were an Angel, I was in heaven last night and it was so beautiful there with wonderful music".

"So you know that you were dead for a few minutes?"

"Yes."

This whole day he was on an euphoric mood, joking with the nurses, planned hunting trips with his brother. He bragged about his grandchildren.

Later in the afternoon, he wanted to have dinner. He had not eaten for a month, now he was hungry and he wanted to have turkey, beer and vanilla ice cream. He had really longed for these.

He enjoyed the dinner, as it was like "Jesus last supper".

He said to the nurse afterwards: "I loved the food-it was like an orgasm".

With my Victorian upbringing, I reacted over his expression:

"What are you saying," somehow very embarrassed. But so he was, straight, natural and spontaneous. The nurse laughed.

In the evening I wanted to go home to eat my dinner.

 He asked me: "stay here with me, baby! " I saw his sad face.

"I'll be back tomorrow morning, my darling.

I love you. "

"Your children will come and visit this evening."

I gave him a kiss and waved to him.

"See you tomorrow, my precious!"

There were no more morning ... ... for him.

I got a call from the hospital 04:45 am, they could not start the heart again and I ran with frosty windows in my car to the hospital, I could barely see through them. I was stressed and rushed up to his room. They still worked on him with CPR, but the doctor said that there is no hope.

 Why? Why?

I wanted to, they would continue with CPR, but the doctor said:

"It is no use, the brain is damaged, because it had no oxygen for an extended period of time. Let's stop the life support machines. "

I have to make decisions for them to stop the machines.

"Please, wait until his daughters have come".

So they did. His daughters came and sat weeping with me around his bed.

6.15 am they shut down the machines. My husband got the most peaceful, beautiful face, no more pain and hopefully a better life now without suffering.

But here we were struggling with the pain and tears of losing a wonderful husband, father, grandfather and brother.

I have suffered a lot with this decision, that the life-support machines would be shut down. I was wondering if this was the right decision.
I am thinking of professor in physics, Stephen Hawkins with ALS, whose wife refused doctors to turn off the machines after he had a stroke, with brain damage and he is still alive.

Anyway, he can't talk, but he has a computer that is connected, so he can write, what he's trying to say. He still gives lectures around the world. I saw the movie about him after Dean's death.

I'm sitting in the chair in the living room and watching Good morning America on television a few days after Dean's death. I hear a very sad birds singing outside of the tree-across from the large window. It is a male-mourning dove, which looks at me and singing. It is the most sad sound I heard from this beautiful dove.

I'm thinking: "you come back and check up on me!"

I start to cry.

"This is a sign from my wonderful husband to come back and check up, how I feel!"

This is so overwhelming and I think there is another life after death. He is there for a long time, to find out how I feel. He is sorry for me, that I'm alone now.

Dean has always been interested in nature and especially birds, he writes about his life in the camp in the desert Wildlife Area, where "thousands of Sandhill Cranes landing within my campsite. All night long their calls deafed the night with screams of birds taken by coyotes and other predators. At dawn their flight to the southern Party took place. It was amazing with thousands of these birds, some coming within 6 m flew up to a vortex. The vortex of birds spiraled up and up until enough altitude was gained to fly south. It was spectular! Most birders wait and watch for years for this amazing display. I was lucky. Right there at the perfect time in the migration. "

16 YEARS BEFORE - Meeting

We met online. We had the nickname in this chat. He was "Sluggo" and I was "Wonder". We had both come into this chat 55+.

You could say, that we were pioneers to meet in this way - in a chat.

We had been in this for a week, when I saw this Sluggo chat with women about his wonderful tulips.

Suddenly, he chatted with me: "I've been in Falun", a Swedish town. He could see, that I was from Sweden in my profile.

This got me interested. Anyone knows Sweden and have been there!

Most were Americans in this chat.

"Oh, you've been in Falun?"

"Yes, I have an aunt there."

"OK."

It was in the beginning and he got me interested. It wasn't true but he wanted my attention and he got it.

There was something in the air - emotions - something very special between us, even though we had the whole Ocean in between. I got feelings for Sluggo. I can't explain it, but I felt so close to him.

In the chat you can "go into a room" to be for yourself, so no one saw, what you chatted about. So we did that.

He said the same thing about me. When he was in this chat, he had feelings for me.

"I am just sitting here looking out over Horse Heaven Hill and reflecting on what has happened to us. It is so wonderful and incredible, that it almost seems to be a "fairy tale". It is like MAGIC.

I have never felt such warmth for any woman. It is almost like you are a missing piece of my life. I try to analyze my feelings. I thought, maybe I am just infatuated, because I need love. No, that was not the case, because I feel so much love from my kids, my family, friends and community. This is special Love. "

Later, I got this Horse Heaven Hills in the State of Washington declared to me. Many horses had been released by indian tribes around 1860. It was like a "horse heaven" for them. They got freedom and plenty to eat. They grew in size, but they destroyed the wheat fields.

There were so many wild horses here in the late 60s. Now, the Government decided to do away with them. They killed many horses and they moved some of them down to Texas.

Dean has read "Secret langauges of relationships", which tells the story from our date of birth, that our relationship is "a miracle of Manifestation".

"You two may approach the relationship a bit like two lost souls, who had some disappointing experences in the road of life, or just oceans due to met the right person.

The mach-up is truly grounding, and the miracle of its manifestation may come as a tremendous relief and great sense of joy for both of you. Crutial here is the sense of trust, for the past has taught both of these partners to keep others at arms length. Just lowering the guard and being relaxed for a while with the other person, can be a great benefit.

Once established this relationship will not only grow but will become most dependable upon one another to the extreme.

Strenghts: Trusting, accepting, established.

Weakness: closed, dependent. "

Sluggo also told me that when he was called up to the army in 1963 for battle in the Vietnam war, he had a vision.

"I was afraid of being killed myself. I had thought of leaving the US and seeking asylum in Canada or possibly Sweden. I prayed to GOD for the answers. My vision was this: I was to someday author of childrens book. This book would give the children of the world a sense of peace and hope. It would enable the children of the world to seek a sense of peace and compassion for others they had been taught to hate. The words for this book are locked in my heart. The vision was, that a wonderful woman, who did not speak my language would un-lock these words of peace. This wonderful woman was my soul mate.

I was so united with hear, at a time, the world needed these words. The vision also stated, that this woman and I would be given an award of peace together. I am now thinking, that this vision will come to pass. I think, that you, precious Wonder, are that woman.

I think, that we have a "mission" to fulfill.

Don´t think I am crazy or unsound. I just think "our"

meeting is unpresidented and so timely. I felt a "warmth"

from you in the first message I recieved. I wish, I could hold

you in this moment. I want to see you and hear your voice.

I know you are "my life". "

USA

It has only been 2 weeks since we met in chat and everything has been overwhelming.

We made plans in e-mail to meet in Los Angeles.

I flew over from Sweden with my two children and we stayed with my daughter in Los Angeles.

Sluggo-Dean would come a week later. We had decided to meet on the Promenade in Santa Monica.

When he arrived in Los Angeles, I told my kids: "I am going to meet a man that I have dated in a month."

"Are you crazy? You do not know anything about him, ", my children said.

Yes, I can understand their frustration over what their mom does.

"Yes, I know, I'm crazy, but if I don't do this, life will be the same.""Loneliness and boring life." I left them to meet my future husband. No idea to explain now. "You will see." "I'm sure it will be fine!"

Dean said to me:

"Your kids love you so much. They are afraid for you and don't want any due harm to come to you. You are so special to them. You feel sad, because they are worried for you. That is so understandable! Because they are so special to you. We then are nervous, because we have such deep feelings of love for each other and can´t really logically explain it for ourselves.

We are then told about the horrible "war" stories of internet love and romance.

People do laugh at these things and are quick to point the absurdities of the whole thing. This is understandable. This is the one of the reasons I have not told very many people about us. I knew, that if I told them, only negatives would be the response. You were in a position of having to tell your children because of our meeting over here.

They are anxious, especially when told details of our "holdless" and "sightless" relationship.

This is so understandable. I would be very sad if your children were NOT worried. "

THE PROMENADE

I'm sitting on the wall outside the shopping center at the Promenade in Santa Monica, where we've decided to get together. I'm nervous, but am happy to soon see my love.

I see a car, that goes around two times with a man in a cowboy hat. It's HE!

Now he will receive me. My Sluggo!

I remember him from the pictures he sent. A big hug.

We decided to eat lunch in a French restaurant on the Promenade.

It's scary the first few minutes in the restaurant. How will this go? Nervous!

We're talking and showing pictures of our children.

We finish lunch and are now starting to walk on the Promenade.

Guess who we met?

My 3 children are coming against us. They are spying on us!

"How are you doing? They don't have a chance to pass without stopping, when Dean greets them.

Dean is so kind to them and they respond politely.

We walk now all together.

CATALINA ISLAND

We have decided to go along, I, my children, and Dean, to Catalina Island the next morning.
All my kids are in a mood of madness, screaming right out, laughing - they are so happy. For me, I think. He was not a strange person but a nice, polite gentleman. They're probably surprised!

We are in a restaurant for lunch. They drink beer and have fun.

We rent a golf car to ride around the island. My children behave the way they really have fun. My son takes photo of trash cans everywhere. Says: "Beautiful!"

Best ride I've ever had with my children and a new man in my life.

It's not so much time for us to go before I go to Sweden.

It is very difficult to separate from each other.

Dean and I had a wonderful week. I moved into his hotel room. We had wonderful dinners with champagne and talked and talked. We visited Hollywood, Beverly Hills, Malibu and all these places I have heard about. On Malibu beach Dean burnt his back, because he was on one side the whole time, looking at me.

The most wonderful passion between us! It was breathtaking to be near him. I knew him with all my body. I heard his bass voice say the most wonderful word. I was stuck in a love for him. We saw the movie "Notting Hill" with Julia Roberts and Hugh Grant. This film turned out to be special for us. So special, so we took the two songs "She" and "You say nothing at all" for our wedding, and these songs are sung by us.

We do not sleep much. Now when we finally met, we wanted to be for each other. Find out who we were, he did not want to make love to me. We have to wait. He gives me a lot of joy, and we are very close to each other. I have so much feelings for my man. We are like two soulmates, that have found each other. The whole Ocean would have been between us, but we all still had feelings for each other. Amazing!

How can this be explained? Or not. Sometimes life is a mystery.

Why we met? On a chat online? We were in the right place at the right time. It was intended that we would meet.

FIRE

I come back to Sweden. Dean writes:

Ï felt smoke coming from north of me. The emergency news radio came on and said, that a large range fire was coming our way. I told all the people living on the slope of Rattlesnake Mtn to prepare for home protection or evacuation, because the fire was coming very fast. I turned in all my irrigation to keep everything wet and opened all fences so livestock could escape. All the men in the area went to cut a fire line. One man had a bulldozer, so we went north and began to cut a line. We worked all night to 0430 this morning. The fire is now under control. There was five different fire departments, the Forest Service and many local fighting this fire. I don't know, any lost homes. But some got minor smoke sickness and minor burns, but not serious. The forest Service came with PBY aircraft and helicopters with water tanks. It was so fearful.

The flames would go 100 meters in the air, when hitting areas, where dead sagebrush had accumalated.

The PBY aircraft would drop water near us as we cut the fire line. This would keep the dry grass wet for our safety. The news radio just said, that 20.000 acres were lost and many cattle and horses. No person was seriosly injured, but several stock children's were lost. "

DEAN TELLS THE FAMILY ABOUT OUR LOVE

"Yesterday was so much stress telling my children about our love and future plans.

I wanted them to know, but I didn't want any pain for them. It went well as I told you.

Dean saying: ¨ Thing is that I love you so much I really feared losing you.

Dean talked to me on phone today.

He is telling me:

"Today was fantastic! I talked with you. Your voice is like beautiful music. I love you so much!

I want to be with you, my love. I want to hold you so close to me and kiss your beautiful lips.

I want to make love to you, my precious. I look at you in the video and my pulse races and my breath leaves me. This is what LIFE is all about.

I know, there will be obstacles, but our love for each other will always carry us through the challenges.

We are meant for each other.

These months seem like a long time but I have waited all my life for you.

You are my true LOVE.

I am so happy and relieved today. We have crossed this obstacle. "

My love tells me.

"I just awakened up by severe thunder and lightning. There is now a fire in Horse Heaven Hills. The emergency radio said, that it is secure within river and burnt out boundaries. There are no homes over there, but I fear for the wild animals. I wish the rain would come! It is ten minutes past from where I am now, so I will stay awake and watch the other country around me. Range fires are a way of life around here in the hot summer. It is natures way of keeping the country clean, but we people live here too. There is a political nature group that says we don't belong here. They say things like, you let the fires burn everything , don't eat meat or plants, they have feelings."

I ask them "maybe you should do what you say, let's not eat plants or animal, let's the fire's burn. It's your bright idea, will you go first?"

I really dislike being sarcastic to other people, but these guys really tax my patience. The thing that is so amazing is that people are for the most part very well educated, masters and PhD's.

I wish they could channel their talents toward more realistic goal ".

Back in Sweden, I get a job in Stockholm. I got a job as a school psychologist. I am aware of the conflicts within the team. It seems, that they blame others for their shortcomings.

"It is amazing, how people can somehow neutralize themselves from a situation, when they are partly to blame.

I can see this in the nature. I have spend a lot of time in the woods and have observed many wild animals behave exactly this way. For instance, the coyote. This is a very intelligent animal. They work together, when things are good. They will share foodkills and protect another coyotes young. When things are bad, the "pecking order" becomes centralized to certain family groups (teachers).

This group now searches out the alone coyote, or smaller family group (the school nurse and psychologist) and steals its food, fights with it and generally makes life unbearable. Now, it is amazing how the university educated people can behave so much like ol' wily coyote. "I wonder what would happen in the coyote community, if the coyotes went to university? Just a different perspective, but non-the-less true. " Dean is writing.

THE MEETING IN SWEDEN

5 months is a long time to be away from each other, when you're in love. I long for my man to come for Christmas. We will be moving to Stockholm in January.

There have been a lot of snow, and everywhere in Sweden you can see electrical candle holders in all windows before Christmas. It's magic!

Arlanda airport, here he is - my Man. A big, warm hug and a kiss on the lips.

WOW, what we have longed for this meeting.

Dean still had jet lag and I heard him go out in the snowy landscape in the middle of the night.

He said to me, he couldn't wait. He was like a child, when he saw all the snow.

He was happy and curious, went around in the small town. He was alone, all asleep, but not he. He met two policemen in a car. They stopped, when they saw him. He did not know why, but he was talking to the police and told them that he had been a deputy sheriff in the United States.

They were impressed and he had a long conversation with them.

Later, he told me about his time as a deputy sheriff in Kings County in Seattle.

He was "undercover" police once, undercover in Hell's Angels gang. He had long hair and long beard and drove a motorcycle. A "Norton" motorcycle he had.

This was a dangerous time together with them and pretending that he was a gang member. He could easily be discovered, that this was not the case.

He kept a distance and had to be very careful. The gang had young teenage girls as slaves and prostitutes in this house. These teens had disappeared from home.

The police's goal was to release these girls from their prison of the house.

He must let police know, when it was time to do it.

When the time came for this action, Dean signaled to the police officers outside to attack the house and gang members. They succeeded very well and got the girls released and gang members were arrested and later imprisoned.

The girls had suffered a great deal as a prostitute. Very sad, what these men had made these young girls.

CHRISTMAS

In Sweden we celebrate Christmas in Christmas Eve and have Christmas dinner and Christmas gifts. It starts all over Sweden with Donald Duck, cartoons from the 60s at 15:00 on TV.

The same procedure each year. It's like a Swedish do not want a change. The same procedure every year. All Swedes in front of the TV at. 15:00.

Dean thought it was wonderful!

"You do this every year?"

"Yes, and we love it".

We had fun with my kids there in the living room, looked on Donald Duck.

My parents arrived for Christmas dinner.

Tradition in Sweden is "smorgasbord" with schnapps. You

have to sing before you can drink schnapps. The song says:

"if he does not take, nor do he half sheep.......".

My son explained to Dean: "you really need to take all, or else you'll get no more.".

Dean thought it concerned all beverages, including wine. So he drank the entire glass of wine in one gulp. He was really drunk, and he was embarrassed that my parents wondered, what a strange human being I had got hold of.

He told me: "It's not easy being in a new country with other traditions and culture." "I was just trying to adapt to the Swedish tradition."

In our little town Gävle the firemen built a big Christmas goat by straw, about 10 m every Christmas. This is a tradition och this goat is very beautiful. Almost every year somebody is burning it down. You can bet on it, if it will burn or not - to win money. For the people in Gävle, it is very sad, when the goat is burning. This Christmas my son had told Dean about this goat, that you can win money, if you burn it down. Later in the end of December the goat is burning. It shows up, that an American man got arrested for burning it down. The other people, who had done this before, have run away. This American did not know, that you could get arrested for it, so he was there, when the Police came.

When I came to my school next morning, the teachers wondered, if my American boyfriend burnt the goat. When

I told Dean about it, he said: " I was close to do it, because your son said, you could win money on it, but I didn´t know that you can be arrested.

CULTURES

We were people from different cultures and traditions.

Dean knew, that Europeans eat with both fork and knife but the Americans only with the fork.

This is difficult for Americans to even use the knife. They cut the meat with a fork. So Dean had practiced that also use the knife, so he would not be noticed as much but thought it was hard and turned back to only using the fork.

He felt like an outsider. My mother noticed that he eats with a fork and offered him a fish knife, because it looked so hard for my mother on the way he ate — only with a fork!

I really like the American way to be very politely received partner. An American man never pass before a woman. He opens the door for a woman, and he opens the car door and lets the woman go first.

If you come as a woman in a corner and meets a man, he takes a step back and let the woman pass first. An American let women sit first on a seat in a bus.

When Dean and I were headed once by bus in Stockholm, we were standing at first, because there were no seats. At the next bus stop, there was some vacant seats and I said: "Come and sit here, Dean."

Dean had his bass voice heard around the bus:

"I never take a seat before the women and children. I will be!"

Suddenly a Swedish man, when he heard my husband, let a woman to sit down on his seat.

Dean was trying to learn Swedish. He went himself to the old town and all of Stockholm to get around himself.

He found, that when he tried to speak Swedish, people responded in English and Swedish people were very good at English.

When he wanted to practice his Swedish in ICA Maxi, a store, once, this came:

He wanted to buy, among other things, olives without pit, but he could not find them.

He asked in Swedish: "I would like to buy olives without pit", ("I would like to buy olives without cock", as it came out in Swedish.) he mixed in pit in the Swedish sense. He did not know the Swedish word for "pit". In Swedish "pit" is a bad word.

The man in the store starts to laugh at him. He did not understand why.

He went home sad and told me that they had laughed at him.

"What did you say?"

"I would like to buy olives without pit" (I would like to buy olives without cock, in Swedish.)

Now, I started laughing and explained to him what he had said. He understood now, why they laughed.

These words that you do not say, because they are in suitable, can be a problem in different languages.

I had the same thing happened to me in the United States. I couldn't understand, why people laughed at me.

I was in a restaurant with my girlfriends. I thought the food at lunch was very good, so I told the waiter:

"Tell the cock, that it was wonderful food."

"Tell the cock (chef =kock in Swedish), that the food was fantastic!"

Everyone laughed and the chef came out and waved to me.

Americans say not, that they go to the toilet. I don't know why, maybe they don't want to tell you, what they are doing in a toilet. They go to the bathroom or restroom. That's all!

For the Swedes, this becomes confused. Once in my sister's house, Dean asked after the bathroom and my brother-in-law asked, if he wanted to take a bath.

Another time, Dean asked about the restroom. My cousin was wondering, if he wanted to rest.

We in Sweden use the word toilet, but the Americans don't use at all the word toilet.

When I punched in my forehead in a cupboard doors in the kitchen, I took a large knife and placed over the forehead, so no bruise would be or swelling, I had learned from my mother. Dean was in the bathroom, I lay down on the bed and had a large knife across my forehead, when he came into the room and saw me.

"I must quickly out of this place. This woman frightens me!" he thought.

Often there were misconception of the confusion of languages or cultural differences. In the beginning there was a problem and Dean said many times, that he would go home to the United States and leave me, but we had the most wonderful proximity, when we sorted out what the problem was.

 We had deeper love after confrontations. I liked Dean's confrontations in some way, although it was difficult many times, he was very straight, hid nothing. He was truthful.

I often wanted to escape from the conflict. I didn't like it, but I learned to stand there and listen to confrontation and say my opinion.

While gone, we've learned from our cultures, what was the obstacle for our love sometimes.

I had shorter and straighter commands sometimes as a Swede, not Dean enjoyed, such as: "Can you go out with the garbage?"

In America they doing the rewrites and is not as direct and sound more friendly.

It may sound, for example: "Would you please...." Could you mind..... "

So when I said,; "You can go out with the garbage?" came to nothing, until I said "Do you mind bring the garbage?" "Can you please go out with the trash...?" Then Dean went out with the trash.

60 's

Dean and I were young in the 60s. We both felt the musical revolution with Elvis Presley, the Beatles, Bill Haley, etc. Our parents protested against the music we listened to. Every Saturday afternoon after school, we went to school on Saturdays, we listened to the Top 10 on the radio.

Parents disapproved of, that we girls screamed for Elvis Presley's hip movements. It was a disgrace, to watch this artist, they found. Beatles guys had long hair, it was unique and sexy.

In the 50´s it had been quiet foxtrot and waltz. In addition, now the girls had skirt up above their knees together with tight Corrêge boots. We had a lot of make-up with black painted with eyeliner on the eyelids at the edge of the eyelashes. In addition, up with teased hair in a backcomb. We would look like Farah Dibah, the Empress from Persia, as it was called then.

Many could make the back comb larger by adding a French bread in. A great deal of hairspray it went to, to keep the hair in place. Keep in mind, when French bread was old, because we did not comb the hair for some days!

Now that Dean and I met, it turned out, that together we could dance rock n´ roll. We had so much fun together and danced to the beautiful music of the 60 's. When we later came to reunion of his graduation from 1962 ,we all danced to the music, which was Top 10 in that year. The reunion was at the top in a house on a cliff overlooking Puget Sound, entrance to Seattle. Beautiful view over the sea and I met all his classmates there.

MARRIAGE PROPOSAL

Dean came back in September to me. We had been apart since the summer, when I had been in the United States with him. The first night he fell down on his knees in front of me and asked:

"Will you marry me?"

For me, this was a surprise and I was thrilled and said:

"Yes!"

He put now a a large diamond ring on my finger.

I was so happy. How could this happen to me!

He hugged me and we stood there like two lost people in a big hug and cried out of happiness.

Now I was "Swede" and told him, that now we need to buy a ring to him, as we do in Sweden, where both have an engagement ring and has a special date for our engagement.

Dean was so sad. This was the way they do in the United States, the man gives the woman he loves a ring and he became very confused, when I talk about a different date, where we will switch rings, as we do in Sweden.

He could not understand this. This was the date he wanted to give me the ring. Another culture crash.

Anyway, we got engaged at the yard to the Finnish Church in Gamla Stan, the old town, where a statue of an orphaned boy was. During the Finnish winter war (1940), many orphaned children came to Sweden and many stayed here in Sweden, after the war was over. This was a monument from this period.

Dean had noticed this place. So he took back his power to decide, that this would be the engagement place. We were happy in our love and the most wonderful engagement dinner in "5 Small Houses" in the old town.

EX

We had partners, who have been unfaithful against us.

For me, it was a horrible thing to find out, that my ex had been cheating on me for half a year. I had known, that something was wrong. I confronted my ex and he told me, that he had a young girl and she was pregnant.

This reality made me so sick for a long time, that a person can be so mean and hide so terrible things for me so far. It was betrayal, that made me sick. I thought we had a good time. My confidence went down.

We were all confused in my family. My ex had a good job and nice children and was happy mostly. He was fond of me.

I analyzed this behavior to understand.

"He chased of course the romantic ideal, but he could not have made a worse choice than the woman, whom he chased with. She had been with many before him probably. It seemed that this woman chose men based on two properties, they must be occupied and must have the status. The fact that it has been part of some mysterious guilt or love safely in a "Pact" with no responsibilities or obligations. My analysis is as follows: the mistress is proud. She has won a victory again. Once again she is Daddy's little girl....... every Daddy's little girl. The first time was just five years old and competed with mom on dad's favor. (Electra complex)

It was the first time she felt triumph.

Once again, she is looking for the drug: to compete with another woman about her husband and to win.

It seems that it is not enough to have a wonderful family, a good job and the economy. It seems like it must be a bit more "exciting", for my ex.

We must keep our illusions in check. Many fantasies are innocent but many are very dangerous.

We need to see the romantic ideal, as they are.

Otherwise they can be like sirens - erotic and tempting - and wave to dangerous waters and self destruction. "

Dean had a similar story with his first ex wife.

He was a deputy sheriff. He worked nights, but this particular evening, he became ill and was driving home.

He was uniformed and had all the guns in the uniform.

He was fully armed, so to speak!

When he came into his bedroom, he found his best friend in bed with his wife.

Uhhhh!

He could have shot this man or both, fully armed as he was.

He shouted: "out of my house, NOW!"

This man got himself quickly out of the house, the fastest way he ever made.

Dean, who for understandable reasons, was very upset, took the police car and drove to his police chief. Where he stayed for a month and the chief made him calmer.

Dean had a hard time getting over this infidelity.

He talked about this betrayal many times.

He also tried to analyze, why this happened.

"both of these best friends had applied for police training in the Police Academy. There were many tests and even physical tests. Dean went through all these. There were thousands who applied but only 100 had to start training. Dean was approved and was admitted to the Police Academy but not his friend. He could see a revenge from his friend to take his wife from him. "

A terrible way to prove his pride to hurt Dean! During this time his wife became pregnant and gave birth to a son - the son unfortunately died after a few weeks. Dean had been   unable to talk about his dead son. He forgot about it.

He also had doubted, whether he was the father.

He was, and the child is named after him and Jr.

For us it was so important to be honest and truthful.

We know that we loved each other so much and did not want to destroy our love.

We were, for several months, because of work, separate from each other. I was in Sweden and Dean in the United States. We had promised each other to be honest and truthful. We both had so many scars from infidelity from our partners.

SEPTEMBER 11 2001

I was in the Gallery near the home. There were people around a TV in the Hall. I stopped and wondered what they looked at.

I saw an airplane flying into one of the World Trade Center towers. All around are quiet.

I do not understand what is happening ..... Now another plane fly into the second WTC Tower. It was a shock. I was wondering ,what happened. I'm calling Dean on the way home. His time was now 6:45am and he still sleeps:

"It's something that happens in New York!" My voice was weak.

"I don't know what it is, two planes have flown into the World Trade Center towers. The Pentagon is also damaged by an airplane "

I could not say anything more, I cried and was scared.

"Huh?"

"I turn on the TV," Dean said .

All evening, I sat on the couch and watch TV and see these airplanes crash into the twin towers. Later collapsing towers, one by one, I see people running for their lives full of dust. "This is surreal!" "What's going on?"

Dean walked into the clubhouse and met the tenants there. Everyone was wondering what's going on. A female neighbor had knocked on his door, cried and was shocked.

Because of the fear of a war, all were home from jobs, many worked in Hanford, nuclear power plant, in the vicinity.

Everyone was here for several days, ordered food, and everyone wanted to be together in this fear.

The world will not be the same after this terrible act of terrorists in America.

United States had blocked all borders from the air. No

aircraft could come over the US border. Dean would 5 days

later fly to Sweden. He was not sure he could do it because

of no flights!

I left early the following morning to be with the children at school and talk to them, about what happened, as a school psychologist. I was in 5th grade. Everyone was very quiet and moved. On the subway out to the suburbs, it was a tense atmosphere, no one said anything and all seemed in shock.

In class, we talked about what had happened, about the two aircraft, which flew into the two WTC towers in New York. I asked them to draw what they had seen on television the night before.

The children also had noticed, how people jump against death from the towers, in their drawings.

I had a Palestinian boy in the class, he refused to draw something.

"No one cares about our suffering in Palestine, why would I be sad, what is happening in USA?" he said.

People wonder what a world we live in. In this awful time, people come close to each other and help each other and join together in grief.

STOCKHOLM

I met Dean at Arlanda Airport 5 days later. We gave each other a big hug, and we were so happy to see each other after this terrible accident in New York and Washington. We hold each other for a long time, glad that we live by this terrible event.

Dean had a lot of anger against the terrorists and people in the Middle East.

We saw a lot of news on the TV and heard how the discussions went in the United States. We watched a lot of CNN.

We understood, that the United States will do something after this humiliation from terrorists. We see, how people in IRAQ are burning the American flag, making Dean very upset.

In January 2003, the United States invaded IRAQ. The Americans wanted to take revenge. Saddam Hussein had been a major sponsor of terrorists. He also killed people of his own.

OUR WEDDING

We have decided to have the wedding in my cousin's old house from 1870, in their dining room. A beautiful house built with towers on the roof, all painted in yellow.

We had prepared this wedding to be a surprise to our family and friends. We had practiced songs from the movie

"Notting Hill," we saw in Santa Monica, when we first met, in months.

I found a long blue dress as a wedding dress. Blue, the most, because I have been married before and blue, because Dean loved me in blue.

I had painted "the blue lady" with a woman dressed in blue, standing by a Rolls-Royse in moonlight. I gave him it and he had it over his bed in the United States. "She is protecting me," he said.

I came up from the basement and stepped into the kitchen, where Dean and the priest was.

"Oh, how beautiful you are, my darling!" Dean said and the priest assented.

All guests now sat in the dining room, and we marched in with the priest in front of us to the tones of Bach.

During the ceremony, we stand with our backs to the audience.

Now we turn against each other.

Dean sings now "She" by Elvis Costello. With his deep bass voice is heard the song out in the big room, and people are very moved and some get tears in their eyes. I sing "You can say nothing at all" by Allison Krauss.

People take photos and I can see that my daughter and my son were very surprised to hear me sing. We are now addresses the audience, see them moved, now that we are listening to "The Prayers" by Charlotte Church and Josh Groban.

When we finish with "Only You" by the Platters, all are so excited!

All are now in an atmosphere of love and joy. We get the champagne out on the lawn. Everyone is happy and we are mostly. Dean gives me the kiss I didn't get during the ceremony.

At last we now are husband and wife.

Dinner is amazing. Italian food and Princess cake and wine.

The dance afterwards - success becomes due. All go running on it, happy and danceable. We have selected the best music from 1962, when Dean graduated. He had received the CD from its last reunion of Graduation.

People had fun, begin to dance rock and roll and jive.

My cousins, he from my mother's side, she from my dad's side, meet again and dancing together after 30 years of reunion. They had a teenage infatuation. In other words, success!

I was so happy to get my husband and he glowed with love in his entire person. He looked at me during the whole ceremony with eyes, that says "I love you so much".

He waited for the priest to say: "you may kiss the bride now", but he said it never.

In Sweden this is not done, but in the United States, it is a custom, to kissing after the ceremony. He was disappointed, but we should have told the pastor before.

Anyway, we were happy, and all of us.

Sluggo got his Wonder, who once met in a chat online.

Can it be more special and strange?!

Now we had the whole wedding night together - alone.

But during the wedding night I had ear ache and was very sick. Early in the morning, I had to go to the emergency room to get a doctor. How can it be so?

BALLOON RIDE

We had had a balloon ride in a gift from all my children.

Now it was time to do it in beautiful June.

It was amazing to observe how they blow up the large balloon with gas. There were about 15 balloons, which were blown up by gas and showed up as pretty colors together.

The basket under the balloon gave room for 22 persons and the captain.

Now, we were all in it and the adventure could begin.

WOW, to see all these houses become less and less, glide over the rooftops, not a sound came from us, just silent gliding. Beautiful landscapes and wonderful to see Stockholm from above.

We surprised people on balconies, as sunbathing and we flew low over them.

Someone shouted in the basket to them: "unexpected visit, Gevalia?"

There is an ad for Gevalia coffee, in which a man falls through the ceiling into a woman's apartment and he says "Unexpected visit, Gevalia?"

Then drink the Gevalia coffee together.

People in motion, when we passing in the baloon, children running after us. On our way down the landing,we turn in a big tree. I get scared and when the balloon comes down on a field, I promptly jumps out of the balloon. The balloon jumps to and fly off again. In the end, landing on adjacent fields.

Now the captain gave us champagne and thanked for the successful flight and we received a diploma.

VIETNAM

Dean has been in Vietnam during 60´. He does not want to talk so much about it. He has awful memories from this time. He saw a lot of bad things. The first time we were living together, he had nightmares. They left in some way when times went by, perhaps he got more secure with me.

He talked with my dad about dad´s experiences of II World War. Anyway, Sweden was neutral but the threat from the Nazis was there the whole time. The trains with Nazis were allowed to pass Sweden to the north to enter Norway, which was occupied by the Nazis.

My dad was drafted during this war. He told Dean things, he never had told me. He was stationed on a island just outside our little town at the Sea. He was there for many months, controlling the sky, the sea, so no foreign boats or airplanes came into Swedish territory. He signaled by semaphor to people on the other islands.

He told Dean, that Europe can thank America, that the Nazis not took over Europe. They all were so happy, when the peace came 1945. Thanks to America!

My dad told him, that he had a Carl Gustav rifle of 1904 during the war.

Dean, who was hunting a lot and had a lot of rifles, now bought a Carl Gustav rifle of 1904. He could sit long times looking at the rifles as Ruger, Beretta, Carl Gustav and admiring the beautiful wood. "This is art for me!", he said.

He cleaned and polished the rifles always after hunting.

Hunting was his passion. There is a tradition in USA to hunt. He told, that he was 12 years, when he first got his rifle and was hunting with his dad and friends. In that time you could bring the rifle to school and put it outside in a box in the hallway.

Think, if this should be now - with all these school shooting in USA!

THANKSGIVING

Dean could come home with deer, pheasant, quail and turkey, which he had hunted.

He was a good chef. He was that one, who made the turkey on Thanksgiving Day. He made it in white wine. He based the white wine into the turkey every hour, so it got to be moisting.

Thanksgiving Day is a very nice tradition. The Americans got it, because when the pilgrims came in about 1600 to America, they got help by the American Natives, the Indians, to find their way. The Pilgrims thanked the Indians with harvest.

For me this was the first time I was invited to a Thanksgiving dinner by his ex wife, children and grandchildren, after I had had breastcancer.

I liked very much, in the way, they thanked for, what has happened during the last year. I thanked the hospital, doctors and nurses, who saved my life and I thanked Dean, who was there for me.

BREASTCANCER

I had 6 months earlier, got to know, that I had breastcancer. It was a shock for me and Dean. When I got to be informed after ultrasound, that I had breastcancer, I only saw Death in front of me. I had my children far away. Dean helped me to look forwards. When everything is over with surgery and radiation, we will go somewhere to enjoy and celebrate, that the breastcancer is gone. He got me to think positive.

I had one month earlier got mammogram in Sweden and everything was ok. When I now got a Health insurance in USA, because I was retired and permanent resident, my family doctor says, that I should have mammogram but I am saying, I have done it in Sweden. "Take it anyway!", he said.

I did that and now there were more investigations as ultrasound and diopsy. Very fast I got surgery to take away a piece in my breast. Dean was there the whole time for me. He comforted me and we cried together. He was so afraid to lose me.

He loved me so much and he wanted to do everything for me, as I would have it well. People came with flowers and greeting cards and gave me support.

When I came into the surgery room, I was very sad and was crying, far away from my children and far away from Sweden, I hear a nurse saying;

"Are you from Sweden?"

"Yes, I am."

"Speak Swedish, though."

Here a Swedish woman is and she is a nurse in a hospital in USA. She comforts me and gives me a hug. I get her phone number and we will meet up later. She became my best friend in USA. I got the most wonderful care by doctors and nurses. My breast cancer has not come back.

I reported the Swedish hospital, which had not seen my breastcancer one month earlier. The report also came to the court, but the hospital defended.

AMERICAN CITIZEN

I became an American Citizen and I made a test about the American constitution and American history. Later I did the Oath and this was a wonderful ceremony. I got the Diploma by the Judge and we sang the American hymn. We got American flags to wave with.

I have now dual citizenships - Swedish and American.

My American friends were very happy, that I am now American citizen. They celebrated me and gave gifts and cards.

SCHOOL

After my retirement I was volunteer in school in our little town in USA. I have a friend, who is art teacher in this school and she asked, if I could help her in the classes.

I had been school psychologist in Sweden and been working with classes and counseling teachers, so this would be fine for me.

It's amazing, how different you are working in schools in the United States against Sweden. This sets the children up on the led and go with the teacher leading the way, as a "duck family" through the corridors. No talking, no screaming. They lined up outside the classroom. The same is done when the kids stop the lesson after drawing an hour. Those who stand silent next to their seats, are now lining up at the door. Class teacher comes and gets the kids.

The children call the teachers with Mrs., Miss, Mr. and not with first name, as in Sweden. It is a disciplined way in the United States to set up on led. The children respect more the adult and it gives a certain distance to teachers is styled with Mrs. and family name. In Sweden the children come on the same level as teachers, when they use first names. This, I think is disrespectful in Sweden and children can easily take over here. I have worked as a school psychologist and seen this with my own eyes.

I have worked in this school for 6 years and it's just as fun, when I get back to the next semester and met by salutation: "good morning Mrs. Kier". I get recognized and they want help to draw and paint.

I enjoy being in the United States. I feel appreciated. They see and hear me here. People always welcome and the cashier at the grocery store always greet and ask, how you feel. "Hi, how are you doing?" I´m doing fine, how are you? " So it is said! It feels good! I would like, that it was more affirmative and positive in Sweden.

There we have the Jante law: "You should not think, that you are anything". I have grown up with this. Children in the United States are encouraged to tell every morning, when they sit on a mat on the floor, what they've done, etc. Teacher takes the time with them and listening to them.

Positive attitude, I think, is the best confirmation, to feel that they are somebody and that somebody hears them. "I am fine as I am."

I can think, that there is a great deal of criticism and negative reviews in Sweden, which one does not feel well off.

Before I met Dean, I dared not eg. set me up and make a speech or as I did in the United States took part in political discussions in the clubhouse. They listened to me here.

Dean encouraged me and not just me, with: "You can do it!"

So I had a speech on my mom's and dad's funeral, in addition to my daughter's wedding.

I heard Dean say: "You can do it!", when the Memorial was to be held for Dean after his death.

So I was speaking at Memorial to him, my beloved, in front of his family and American friends.

After Dean´s death I met a woman from Tibet in the clubhouse. I told her, that Dean had passed away. She got very sad and cried. Dean had talked a lot to her husband and her in the clubhouse. Dean was sad to see, how the man treated his wife. She was not allowed to talk, she was walking after him. One time he told the woman to walk to store herself to learn English and understand English. "You can do it !", he said.

Now the woman told me: " I did as your husband told me to walk to store alone and I now understand more English. He was so good, your husband".

When Dean was here in Sweden, he talked a lot, as Americans do, and the Swedes don't break in, so he was talking very unchallenged. He was very verbal and he spoke in English, of course, which he mastered. I can see, that Americans have a very good self-esteem.

When Dean came down to the bus stop in Sweden, he said at the beginning: "Hi, how are you doing?" to people there, but he rarely got a response. He began to believe, that it was wrong for him. I told him, this is Swedish way, not to talk to strangers. At the same time as they were shy or …

Dean praised me a lot. I, like a Swedish, was not used to this. Many times, he said. "How beautiful you are!" "No, I am not." He thought, that it was weird, that I could not receive a compliment. It was once again the Jante law with me: "You should not think, that you are anything!" Finally he said to me: "say, thank you!", when you receive a compliment, and I have learned now, to thank for a compliment, for Americans are easy to give compliments. They have also much easier to say: "I love you!" than we Swedes have. It sounds beautifully and I am happy about that. My answer would be: "I love you too!" This feels good. The Americans also say: " Nice to meet you!", when you get introduced to them. It sounds so good.

SWEDISH IN THE UNITED STATES

One evening, we had been to dinner with friends, this
happens. On the way home we went through the dark desert,
not a car on the road. Suddenly, I hear Dean saying to me in
Swedish: "Go home to bed!" in an accent of Swedish talking
in the North. I was so pop. Who speaks my language in the
middle of the desert? It turned out, that Dean had courted his
girlfriend and become a little too long in her house, when
the girl's grandmother from northern Sweden, living in the
United States, said to Dean: "Go home to bed!"

At our countless parties around the pool, in the middle of
our housing complex, Dean had taught a Canadian man the
expression: "Go home to bed!" in Swedish. When my
daughter was visiting and swimming in the pool, she hears
a man in swimming pool say: "Go home to bed!". In
Swedish! She will be just as surprised, as I was, to hear
Swedish in a pool in the United States.

Our BBQs around the pool was very nice. Many Canadians,
Russians etc and Americans met there, to eat together. The
practice is, that everyone brings something to BBQ, salad,
corn on the cob, meat etc.

Some evenings in the summer, it may be up to 40 degrees C.
When it's so hot, it's just swimming pool or AC in the
apartment, as applicable.

I had very hard for this blazing heat. I was new to it, stopped any time indoors or bathed in the swimming pool or the jacuzzi. When I was shopping, I stayed close to the deal, so I did not have to walk far in the heat.

DYSLEXIA

I was educated in Dyslexia. I did assessments of children and diagnosis and made action program.

Dean was dyslexic and through him, I learned practically, what it's like to be dyslexic.

A dyslexic person cannot remember for a long time, what has been said, have weak short-term memory, forgetting fast. Dean then put up notes on the door, what he would remember. He repeated often loud, what he would do. He listened to everything instead of reading. In elementary school the teacher had scolded him because he did not take, what he would do. He was many times be ostracised, for he could not do, what the teacher wanted. It was all about his dyslexia, he had lost the information, what he would do because of weak short-term memory.

In high school, teachers understood his problems with reading and writing, He was listening now to the teachers in history and other topics and could now store all that the teachers told. His rating was raised, because now he could store all learning by listening. He was a master of remembering and usually he could all responses on "Who wants to be a Millionaire".

To cope with and to be police at the Police Academy was a triumph for him. Similarly, to be an engineer and then working at Boeing in Seattle.

If teachers could understand, how hard these children, have in school, when they are dyslexic or have other diagnoses such as ADHD. How many have not received the low self-esteem by teachers, who do not understand them. A teacher would teach, how dyslexics learn, usually through to see photos by learning. A dyslexic is more of a picture person. It notices more details than the whole. The traditional learning in school is reading and then reading is a problem for dyslexic. There are other ways, as image and to listen to the content, to help the dyslexic. A dyslexic has bigger right brain, which features such as analytical, technical, mathematical, creative ability exists. Therefore, they are skilled in computer, technology etc. In the left hemisphere is the reading and writing skills - this hemisphere is less of dyslexic, which explains that he gets more difficult for reading and writing.

DISEASE

The first time I was with, when Dean had a heart attack, was in Stockholm. I was at my school psychologist head of the annual wage talk. The secretary comes in and says, my daughter called and said, that Dean had a heart attack and is headed by ambulance to the hospital. I am, of course, very afraid and I asked to go to my husband. My boss thought, that I could remain until the hour was over but I didn't. This was the question of life or death. When I enter in the hospital, he is connected with machines and oxygen supply. My daughter is already there and soon my two other children are coming.

Later they made an angiogram, angioplasty of vein near the heart.

Dean told, that he had his first heart attack when he was 42 years old. He then worked as an engineer at the Hanford Nuclear plant. He had a good job and good pay.

Now, he does not work anymore, then they were afraid, that he could get a new heart attack. As hard as it was, that he was sick paid from his work. Family with 3 children were struggling financially.

He has had about 14 heart attacks but every time he survived, when skilled doctors did angiogram and angioplasty.

He had both done a bypass surgery and 3 years before he died, he had a defibrillator. a type of AED. Dean was a fighter. He was a tough hospital patient and knew a lot about his medical conditions. It was very concerned many times, when he said to me: "call the ambulance, I think I had a heart attack".

Countless times he was in the hospital but came home. We tried to live as usual. We made trips to Paris, Mallorca and resorts in Sweden.

Health care system in the United States does, that it is very expensive to be in hospital. It costs a lot. You have to have a good health insurance, Dean had a health insurance, which paid 80% of health care costs. It did, that he was drawn with debts after every time, he was into hospital.

The last half of the year Dean got dialysis. His kidneys had been destroyed by the countless times they had injected contrast in his veins, when x-rays or angiogram would be made.

Every day he went to Dialysis Center and got dialysis. Later, he did the dialysis at home. He was capable to wash all hoses and give himself dialysis. Wonderful people around were for him - doctors, nurses and friends.

Dean knew, that he hadn´t so long time left. He wanted me to move back to Sweden, if he passed away. He warned me, that ISIS can take over Europe and Sweden. He thought Swedish people were too blue eyed and thought good about every refugee, but Sweden had let in too many refugees.

"They can take over." "Soon you are walking in a burka," he said. You can come over to USA, whenever you want. You are an American Citizen. Also your children can come here, when they now got permanent visa through me. This he said in 2014 and now we have had terror attacks in Europe and threats in Sweden. My husband could feel far away, what could happen. Many times it was true, what he had said. It would be awful, if he is right, that terrorists or ISIS take over us.

Now it was over for him. He had survived so many times, but now it was his Life's end.

He was loved by many! I will love you forever, Dean! I miss you so much!

This was Match made in Heaven, so we will meet again in Heaven. I truly believe that!